AMATA MEANS BELOVED

AMATA MEANS BELOVED

Sister Mary Catharine Perry, O.P.

✝

Sr Mary Catharine Perry. op

iUniverse, Inc.
New York Lincoln Shanghai

Amata Means Beloved

iUniverse, Inc.

For information address:
iUniverse, Inc.
2021 Pine Lake Road, Suite 100
Lincoln, NE 68512
www.iuniverse.com

Cover photograph: Sr. Judith Miryam of the Trinity, O. P.
Illustrations: Monastery of Our Lady of the Rosary, Summit, New Jersey

Ring the bells by Leonard Cohen is from: *Patches of Godlight,* Jan Karon, Penguin Books, New York, NY, 2001.

ISBN: 0-595-30024-3

Printed in the United States of America

Let Him be placed in complete possession of your heart who for love of you was placed upon the Cross.

St. Augustine

For my sisters

…and Betty

…and Betty

ACKNOWLEDGEMENTS

With gratitude to the sisters of my religious community for their support and encouragement. Sister Maria of the Cross, O.P. what would I do without your superb editing and unhesitating use of the red pen? To the two Betty's in my life who encouraged me to write: Elizabeth Paulin, my first writing teacher way back in eighth grade and Elizabeth Kuhns, with whom corresponding via e-mail rekindled my long ago desire to be a writer "when I grow up"; to Julia O'Sullivan, whose friendship and never-ending font of ideas has brought joy to my life; to my family, for their love and support. Most of all, I thank God for the precious gift of my Faith, for the gifts He has continued to bless me with, and most especially, for the gift of being a spouse of Christ Jesus as a Dominican contemplative nun.

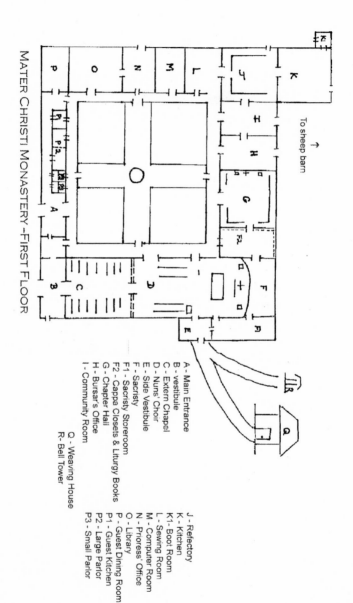

MATER CHRISTI MONASTERY –FIRST FLOOR

To sheep barn →

A - Main Entrance
B - vestibule
C - Extern Chapel
D - Nuns' Choir
E - Side Vestibule
F - Sacristy
F1 - Sacristy Storeroom
F2 - Cappa Closets & Liturgy Books
G - Chapter Hall
H - Bursar's Office
I - Community Room

J - Refectory
K - Kitchen
K1- Boot Room
L - Sewing Room
M - Computer Room
N - Prioress' Office
O - Library
P - Guest Dining Room
P1 - Guest Kitchen
P2 - Large Parlor
P3 - Small Parlor

Q - Weaving House
R- Bell Tower

Nuns at Mater Christi Monastery at the time of Emily's entrance:

Sister Blanche Marie of the Trinity-Prioress
Sister Ossana of the Annunciation-Sub-prioress-Bursar
Sister Maria Bernadette of the Rosary-Novice Mistress
Sister Mary Elaine of the Holy Spirit-Farm
Sister Maria Christine of Jesus-Weaver
Sister Mary Dominic of the Eucharist-Head Chantress
Sister Catherine Cecilia of the Mother of God-Sheep manager
Sister Mary Jordan of the Nativity-Kitchen
Sister Maria Christi-Temporary Professed-Sacristan

Sister Regina-Extern Sister

Sister Zita Anne of the Passion-Novice

May the Word of God dwell in you richly.
Colossians 3:16

CHAPTER I

It was their motto that grabbed her: *Veritas*, Truth.
And wasn't that what gnawed and ate at her deep down:
What really was the truth? Were things so black and white
and simple as all those at the lay community made it seem?
Her mind glanced over the fifteen years her family lived as
part of a community of Catholic families. It wasn't the cul-
tic and extreme place that many who misunderstood made
it out to be. There was a lot of fun, a sense of stability, a
sense of knowing what was right and what was wrong.

Emily continued walking down the road. She had convinced the man who drove the limo service car from the
airport that she could carry her suitcase herself. After all,
they all had wheels now. She didn't want him to know
where she was going, although at the last minute she had
almost blurted it out. Sort of like having one last person
this side of the wall know before she did it. Like when
reporters interviewed people who said, "I talked with her

3

Monday at 9:40 or so and this evening on the news I was shocked to hear she had *disappeared!*"

It wasn't quite so dramatic. She had come here so many times in the past two years that it was almost familiar. Yeah, familiar. What about *her* family? Was she walking away from them? Or was she—?

The tears began rising up. "Stop it, Emily!" she ordered herself. "Not now. Later. Think!"

Emily looked up and through her tears saw the sign. "Welcome. Mater Christi Monastery. Founded 1998." She was here. "Keeping walking. Don't stop."

Emily realized she was getting tired of lugging her suitcase behind her. She turned into the long driveway leading up to the entrance of a simple, white building with a cross jutting up from the roof. The novice mistress, Sister Maria Bernadette, had once told her that the cross had come from a monastery that closed at about the same time they were building theirs.

Opening the wooden door, Emily's eyes adjusted from the bright September sunlight to the dark interior. At a desk to the left was an older sister talking on the phone, or rather, being talked to, it seemed. It was Sister Regina, the community's extern sister, who took care of the outside business of the monastery, leaving the cloistered sisters free to devote their days to what they came for: prayer and praise in the midst of a close-knit community life. Sister Regina was a part of the community, of course. She lived in the cloistered area and took her meals with the other sisters and prayed the hours of Lauds, Vespers, and Compline with them. Sister Regina caught sight of Emily and her face lit up with the radiant smile that captured the hearts of the monastery's visitors and benefactors. When Sister Regina had been young she had been a model, made lots of money, and had been on the covers of top fashion magazines. Her story was on the *inside* of the same magazines when word got out what Laura Reynolds had decided to do with her life at forty-one! Most *mags* got the whole story wrong, but even after fifteen years Sister Regina would occasionally get a call from a writer wanting a story.

After a few hasty words to the person calling, Sister Regina walked quickly toward Emily, enfolding her in a warm affectionate hug:

"Welcome, Emily! Well, you made it! Scared? It's OK. That's normal. Hey, thank God we have a normal postulant!"

Sister Regina looked deeply into Emily's eyes and gave her a squeeze.

"You won't feel so alone, once you're in there. I promise. In six months you'll be wondering if you ever lived anywhere else! Look, why don't I call in to Sister Blanche Marie. They've been expecting you. Come on, sit down and take a deep breath!"

Striding over to her desk, Sister Regina picked up the phone.

"Sister? Yes, is Sister Blanche Marie there? Emily is here. What? No, not too much. Three? How 'bout four. One plain. All right, four large pizzas on their way! Yum.

I can't wait. OK, sure. I'll bring her to the small parlor right away. Yes, Sister, I know how to do it. Did it myself, don't forget. Yes, God be praised forever!"

Sister Regina caught sight of Emily's surprised look out of the corner of her eye and inwardly smiled. They were all alike, these women who came to cast their lives before God, to live the radical call of the Gospel that couldn't be silenced. She remembered her own surprise the day that she entered the monastery; entered a community that formed and nurtured her vocation for ten years, before they decided that the best way to invigorate the charism of their monastery was to close: a small remnant of sisters would form a new monastery, more in keeping with the spirit of their rule and constitutions. *Her* entrance day they'd had a popcorn and ice cream party on the cloister. Like Emily, she had thought naively that such simple treats had disappeared from her life forever!

Pizza was a treat, a dispensation from the strict fast they had brought back as a monastic observance. Sister Blanche Marie and the other ten sisters knew how Emily had struggled to pay her college debts and convince her family that this decision to become a cloistered nun was truly God's will. As devout as they were, it was hard work convincing them. Emily needed an extra warm welcome. Besides, that nice man who owned the pizza place, Fred Martino, insisted that *anytime* the sisters wanted pizza, it was on the house.

Pizza wasn't important right now, Emily's entrance ceremony was. Emily found herself suddenly shivering and feeling clammy all over. "What if I faint?" she asked herself. She never had before, but there was always a first time. She looked up and caught sight of Sister Regina's calm demeanor. "I wonder if she felt like I do now, when *she* entered," Emily found herself wondering.

"Emily, Sister Blanche Marie says I'm to bring you to the small parlor. OK?"

Emily followed Sister Regina through the little corridor to the parlor.

"I feel like a seven year old kid," she said to herself. "Like that time I got called into Mother's office for shooting a rubber band at the blackboard when Sister Mary Loretta had her back turned."

She was surprised at herself. She never expected to feel so awkward, so scared.

The parlor was only a few steps from the vestibule and suddenly Emily found herself before a wooden door. She dimly recalled that Sister Mary Elaine had once told her that the enclosure doors at the old monastery did not have door-knobs on the outside. The urge to run out, to keep running madly down the road and catch up with the limo driver overwhelmed her.

"O Jesus," she prayed silently, "please, don't let me make a big mistake. If this is what YOU want I want it, too. Help me."

The door opened and standing there in front of her were Sister Blanche Marie and Sister Maria Bernadette.

"Welcome home, Emily. Welcome to Mater Christi Monastery."

She gave Emily a large, generous hug and Sister Maria Bernadette followed after her. "Come on in, Emily. Let's get you settled while we have time before Vespers. I have your cell already, the one looking out to the garden."

Sister Maria Bernadette put her arm around Emily and led her towards the part of the house called the novitiate reserved for those in formation. It was small like most of the monastery, and like the rest of the house it was bright, austere yet welcoming. It was peaceful—a place of prayer.

Horarium of Mater Christi Monastery

Rise 3:45

Matins 4:00

Lectio Divina, **and Prayer, pick-up Breakfast 4:30-6:00**

Lauds 6:00

Farm Chores

Mass 7:15

Followed by Thanksgiving

Study 8:15-9:00

Terce 9:00

Work (translating/weaving house/household duties)

Classes in Novitiate

Rosary and Sext 11:30

Dinner 12:00

Recreation 1:00-2:00

Siesta

None 3:15

Chapter on Fridays

Work (including Farm Chores in winter)

Vespers 5:00

Private Prayer 5:30-6:00

Collation follows

(Farm Chores in summer)

Compline 7:00

Lights out 8:30

The main purpose for your having come together is to live harmoniously in your house, intent upon God in oneness of mind and heart.

Rule of Saint Augustine

CHAPTER II

Emily stood looking out the window at the stars glistening in the sky. The silence of the darkness seemed to carry the world into timelessness. Emily waited. Soon, Sister Mary Elaine, the bell ringer for the week, would walk up and down the dormitory hallway, swinging her bell, determined that no sister would oversleep. The enveloping silence would shatter and Emily would hear the clank, clank of the rising bell in the distance. During her first days in the monastery, Emily would be awakened by the sound echoing across the quadrangle from the professed sisters' wing. Now, she often slept through it. As a newcomer, a postulant, Sister Maria Bernadette would not permit Emily to attend Matins at 4 AM and told her that she was to sleep until 5:30 to be up in time for Lauds at 6:00. For the past three months Emily did just that.

This morning was different. Yesterday, after Vespers, Sister Maria Bernadette informed her that she could rise this morning for Matins for the Solemnity of the Immaculate Conception:

"We'll see; if you don't spend the day yawning, perhaps we'll consider letting you rise for Matins on the big feasts while you are a postulant."

Excited by the anticipation of participating in another community function, Emily rose before the bell. She didn't like the sound of the bell: it brought back things too painful to think about. At least they didn't have a "real" bell tower. Emily recalled the startled, quizzical look on Sister Ossana's face during her first visit to the monastery while talking to the sisters in the parlor. Trying to act as though the question was of no importance, Emily had asked if they had a bell tower.

"No, we don't," the sub-prioress had said, "but we'd love to have one. Our monastery is new and we finished the basic parts of it right before the war when the economy went plunging. It's out of the question now. You're probably disappointed, right? I mean, doesn't a *real* monastery have a bell tower?"

"Oh, no sister," Emily had quickly answered. "I don't mind at all. I prefer it."

"You do, huh? Well, that's a change." And she'd left it at that.

*   *   *

Emily knew she needed more time than the sisters to dress for Office. The sisters wore the habit to bed, only needing to throw on the veil and slip their feet into socks and sandals before Matins. Later, before Lauds, they would don their day habits. Emily however, had to fully dress in her three-quarter length gray skirt and dark blue smock blouse and short veil. She couldn't wait for the day when she too, would wear the white Dominican habit.

Sister Maria Bernadette had hinted that the community might consider giving her the habit in March:

"We *may* give you the habit in March, dear. You know the community has to vote. You've made much progress in many ways but you still have to learn many things. Most of all you have to learn to relax, to let your sisters love you, to love them in return. The community is where God shows His love for you and where you show your love for Him. Relax. Don't feel you have to work so hard to belong. Friendship is important in our Dominican tradition; try not to be so distant."

Bundled up against the cold in her thick Irish sweater, Emily pondered on what the novice mistress had said. She sighed. Sometimes, it was hard not to be discouraged. Sometimes, everything about the monastery seemed upside-down, a paradox, inside out.

Having been raised in a traditional Catholic family, Emily, Sister Emily now, was used to obeying the rules. Obeying the rules meant you were being good. Didn't being good mean you were also trying to be holy?

Just two months in the monastery and the nuns had shown her another way.

"Yes, we do try to obey the rules," Sister Blanche Marie patiently said one day while the two of them were going for a walk in the woods on a late day in November. "After all, in our way of life, many of our rules are decided by the community. We'd be rather stupid if we ignored the rules we made ourselves. Our life is more than obeying rules, though. So much more."

Sister Blanche stopped and continued walking, sliding her feet through the wet, fallen leaves on the path.

"Sister, I know that. I mean I thought I knew that, but when I'm confronted by Sister Mary Elaine or annoyed by Sister Zita Anne, I feel that unless I control myself, keep my mouth shut and work to please them, I'll be told to leave!"

Sister Emily gave the wet leaves a hard kick, sending a clump flying in the path.

"Emily, you're not here just to 'get along' with the sisters, right?"

The prioress turned toward Emily expecting an answer.

"I know, but..." Emily's voice trailed off in exasperation. Why did she sometimes feel that she was always up for approval? Wasn't she?

Sister Blanche read through Sister Emily's sigh.

"Sister Emily, I know you feel that we all watch you giving you marks of disapproval or approval. Today Emily gets a 9! Yesterday a 7! We all felt that way at the beginning. Of course, you are going to get along better with some sisters than with others. That's only natural. But it can't stop there, can it?"

She waited to complete the thought, teasing it out of Emily.

"Yeah, you're right. Are you trying to tell me that I've got to think a lot more about pleasing God and less about pleasing Sister Mary Elaine when she insists that the lettuce must be covered with a wet cloth in just the correct way?"

"What do you think?"

"I guess it boils down to: why did I come here? Is that what you are trying to get at?"

Emily turned her dark brown eyes straight at the Prioress' face. All the earnestness of her twenty-three years was focused on Sister Blanche. "She means business," Sister Blanche Marie thought. "Good. She's not a jelly fish; not that I ever thought she was."

"Bingo, Emily! That's just what I'm getting at. Why did you come here? Is the answer the same as when you first called us on the phone and insisted on coming to see us? Or is it different?"

Sister Emily hesitated to answer. It was hard putting all this into words. She took a deep breath that was audible even to Sister Blanche Marie and stammered.

"Yes, I'm here...no, it's different...I mean, this whole vocation thing is bigger than I thought. What I'm trying to say is that, yes, my reasons for coming to the monastery are the same, sort of, but they're different, too."

"OK, one step at a time. When you first called us, why did you want to become a nun?"

"Bottom line? I fell in love with Christ at a retreat at college. Not that I was some sort of lazy Catholic before. You know that. This was different. I fell in love. I wanted to give my whole life to Jesus, to be His…"

Sister Emily's voice trailed off. It was hard talking about something so personal and so intangible yet so sure…to herself.

"Good. But what about now? You're not in love, anymore?" Sister Blanche teased.

"Of course I am, Sister!" Emily kicked another clump of leaves. "Are you kidding?"

"I'm kidding. Go on."

"Now, I'm wondering how selfish I really was. It's not just me-and-Jesus, you know?"

"Keep talking."

"I guess I just assumed that I would get along with all the sisters because we were here for the same purpose. That it would be easy to love them. I mean, of course I didn't always get along with my brothers and sisters, but that's normal. Now I'm beginning to see that life in the monastery is more about loving God *through* loving the sisters, especially the ones that annoy me. And….and…."

Sister Blanche Marie continued encouraging Emily along.

"Go on. And, what? Come on, it's OK."

She gave Emily a big hug and rubbed her back affectionately.

"Well, I wanted to give my life to God because I felt that's what He wanted. I wanted to live my life in such a way that it had real meaning. You know, look back on my life at eighty and feel like I didn't waste it. Of course, my dad thinks I am wasting it doing this but let's not get into that."

"At least he isn't against your vocation. He just thinks that with the world in the state it is right now, you could be of better service to the Church by joining an active community of sisters."

"Right. What was I saying? Oh, well, after the terrorist attack of 9-11 and after my brother was killed at the seminary in Denver I began to see that prayer was more important than I ever realized. The best way I could make a difference in this crazy world was to pray for it. Protests and active resistance aren't my cup of tea. But I could pray. I could offer my life for the world."

"Are you still convinced of that now?"

"Yes. The difference is that now I'm starting to realize that it's these little everyday things, you know, the picky stuff, like making sure the towels are hung right to dry in the laundry, or that I cover the lettuce exactly the way Sister Mary Elaine *thinks* it should be covered, or taking my turn to help Sister Ossana with stacking wood for the stoves—I never realized how important all that is in the eyes of God as a way of praying for the world!"

"It's awesome, wouldn't you say?"

"Yeah, scary, too. I mean, do you know how selfish I am?"

Emily smiled at Sister Blanche Marie. This conversation was beginning to take a weight off her. She needed this.

"Welcome to the human race, Sister Emily. A little more self-knowledge like that and you'll do fine here. Come on. We have twenty minutes before Vespers. We just might have time for a cup of tea."

*   *   *

Clang. Clang. Clang. Emily was shaken out of her reflecting by the rising bell. She shivered and involuntarily hugged herself. She whispered to the dark,

"I won't forget, Dan. I offer this for you."

The nuns first build up in their own monasteries the Church of God which they help spread throughout the world by the offering of themselves.

Constitutions of the Nuns of the Order of Preachers.

CHAPTER III

Emily quickly learned that the day-to-day life of the nuns of Mater Christi Monastery differed little from the routine of the first nuns gathered together by St. Dominic in 1206. Eight hundred years she thought in wonder: eight hundred years of rising in the early morning to pray in silence, to praise God by singing the Psalter, to ponder and study the Word of God. Eight hundred years of working to make a living, but not in such a way that it overpowered their lives of contemplation. For eight hundred years, generations of women had committed themselves to living this special kind of community life following the Rule of St. Augustine, one of the most influential of the Church Fathers.

The basics were the same, Emily found, but in many ways life at Mater Christi was radically different. While the nuns who founded the monastery were determined to rededicate themselves to many ancient monastic practices that had fallen by the wayside in recent years because of

the lack of able-bodied sisters, they were also determined
to accept the reality that they were living in a technologi-
cal age. The 21st century was here to stay.

The monastery was simple in design; they had early on
decided to keep the monastery size small enough that the
upkeep wouldn't be a threat to their meager, unreliable
resources. Such a decision was a blessing as the economy
quickly spiraled downhill shortly after the monastery was
completed. The unexpected burning of oil fields in Iraq
and Kuwait meant fuel was only for the wealthy. The nuns
took one look at their one hundred and seventy-five acres
of woodland and consulted experts on the best way to use
their resource and still propagate new forest growth.
Shortly after, they installed wood stoves in the main rooms
of the monastery including the nuns' choir.

Solar panels gave much needed electricity several
hours each day. Unknown to most, even other members of
the world wide Order, the new Pope, a Dominican friar
himself, had entrusted to the community the translation of
papal documents. As a young friar he had been a frequent
visitor to the nuns at the old monastery, coming to give
them lectures in theology, and often asking them to help
with book projects. The new monastery had immediately
come to his mind shortly after his election as Pope when
he needed someone he could trust to translate a particularly sensitive letter. While many contemplative monasteries balked at the idea of internet access, the nuns at Mater
Christi accepted the technology calmly. With solar power
electricity, the fact of an ocean separating them from the
Holy Father was irrelevant.

The sisters had chosen to be strict about newspapers and magazines coming into the monastery. Daily, the "Communications Sister" posted a summary of the day's news on the bulletin board. Events continued to happen so quickly both in the USA and around the world it was sometimes difficult to figure out just what was going on.

As generous as the Pope was to the community, it wasn't enough to pay the bills and put food on the table. Shortly after the sisters began building their monastery, the state had passed a law rescinding the tax-free status of religious communities such as theirs. The added burden of paying taxes on their land meant the nuns needed a loop-hole. A good friend who was a lawyer investigated and told the sisters that if they farmed half of their land, they would be able to qualify for tax-free status under an environmental-agricultural law.

Reaction was initially mixed. As much as they needed to keep their land tax free, most of the sisters were from cities or suburbia and doubted they could keep a farm. Sister Mary Elaine and Sister Catherine Cecilia were the exceptions. So, because these two sisters had some farming experience—Sister Mary Elaine's family ran a farm in the Midwest and Sister Catherine Cecilia had worked on a fruit farm during her summers while in college—the community decided to give the venture a try.

Since Sister Maria Christine had a degree in textile design from Rhode Island School of Design, and since much of the land was open fields, raising sheep and creating a line of hand-woven products seemed an obvious choice. The old barn on the property was renovated to become their weaving house. With electricity at premium, the bright multi-windowed room made it possible to do much of the work without extra lighting. With help from several benefactors the sisters invested in four production looms and created a line of beautiful, yet practical coverlets under the title of "Golden Run Blankets." Golden Run was the creek that ran through the property. As the friars who served the monastery as chaplains and confessors went back and forth from their priory in New York City to Mater Christi Monastery, they introduced the nuns' blanket line to shops in the city. In time, the monastery built up a stable clientele which in turn provided a steady source of income.

*   *   *

For Emily, it was exactly this unique blend of tradition and technology, old and new that attracted her to the newly established monastery. After the retreat that had become the catalyst toward a contemplative vocation, Emily had enlisted the guidance of one of the chaplains on the campus. Emily was familiar with Sisters, of course—she'd had them for twelve years in Catholic school. But contemplative nuns? Which ones?

Father Hilary, a Dominican Friar and an experienced director, suggested that Emily make a commitment to spend time each day before the Blessed Sacrament, asking Christ to show her where He wanted her to live out her vocation as His spouse:

"If He is calling you to religious life He has just the right place for you. When the time is right He'll show you, I promise you that. Meanwhile, pray."

For some of the students at the college that initial advice might have seemed a frustrating answer, but to Emily it was the first thing to do. Praying the rosary at night, sometimes dropping off to sleep in the middle, had been a part of Emily's life since her First Holy Communion. With college and a part-time job to pay for it, finding extra time to spend in the college chapel wasn't always easy, but these times of prayer became the support of her whole day. One day, Father Hilary handed her a sheet of paper with the names and addresses of various monastic orders:

"Get acquainted with some of these monasteries. The Holy Spirit will do the rest."

Benedictine, Carmelite and Poor Clare monasteries were the obvious first choices but after making preliminary contact with their vocation directresses none seemed to respond to the wordless yearning and deep questions of her heart. Perhaps she didn't have a contemplative vocation after all? Father Hilary encouraged Emily not to give in so easily. Strangely, he had failed to tell her about the cloistered nuns of his own Order. One morning, a classmate who was also thinking of becoming a nun handed her a small booklet entitled "Do you wish to follow Christ?" It was the vocation brochure of Mater Christi Monastery. One glance and Emily knew "This is where I want to go!"

The Lord grant that you may observe all these precepts in a spirit of charity as lovers of spiritual beauty, giving forth the good odor of Christ in the holiness of your lives; not as slaves living under the law but as women living in freedom under grace.

Rule of Saint Augustine

CHAPTER IV

"Staying cooped up in here on a cold January day with the wood stove crackling out its heat is one thing, but on a June day like this—that is another thing altogether!"

Emily grasped the beater on the loom, giving the blanket she was weaving a definite *whamp*!

"Come on, Emily, knock it off!"

She wasn't Emily anymore; she was Sister Maria Amata of Christ. She still thought of herself as Emily. She talked to herself as Emily. She was doing it now.

The conversation with Sister Blanche Marie in November proved to be the catharsis Emily, Sister Maria Amata, needed. Slowly, she began to relax and to open up to the community. Her vocation was blossoming. Still, the sisters sensed a certain reticence in Emily. When she thought no one was noticing, Emily, usually cheerful among the sisters, gave way to sadness.

The community knew about the murder of her brother Daniel at the seminary, of course. The story had been all over the news when a group of them were killed by a man who suddenly walked into the seminary one day and began shooting anyone in sight. He then turned the gun on himself. No one knew what his motive was.

What part Dan had played in the sad drama none of them knew. "Please, I'd rather not talk about it," was Emily's response. As part of the application process to enter, a group of sisters—the Council—had interviewed her in the parlor. Sister Mary Dominic had asked her if she had any brothers or sisters and Emily's eyes had filled with tears.

"I have two younger sisters, a younger brother...an older brother...he was in the seminary...the one in Denver...he was killed in the rampage a year later. Please, I'd rather not talk about it."

*   *   *

On March 25, the Solemnity of the Annunciation of the Lord, Emily prostrated before the prioress and community in the chapter hall and asked to be received into the community and receive the habit of the Order of Preachers, the Dominicans.

"Emily Barone, what do you ask?"

The prioress addressed the question to the blue and gray figure stretched out in the form of a cross on the floor.

"I ask for God's mercy and yours."

"Rise."

Emily removed her gray skirt and blue blouse as Sister Blanche and Sister Maria Bernadette enveloped her in the white tunic and scapular of the Order. The leather belt, rosary and white veil completed the habit. The black *cappa* or mantle was then placed over her shoulders. The black veil would come later at first profession.

Only at the very end of the simple ceremony did the community learn the new name Emily would receive.

"Emily Barone, you will be known as Sister Maria Amata of Christ.

*   *   *

During the retreat preceding the ceremony, Sister Maria Bernadette had asked Emily what name she would like to choose.

"I'm still really not sure, Sister. Can you believe it? Sister Mary Dominic told me once that she knew what name she wanted even *before* she entered the monastery! She said she took it as a sign to enter when she learned that the old Sister Mary Dominic had died just the month before!" Emily had wrinkled up her nose in disgust. "Sorry, that's not my thing!"

Sister Maria Bernadette, never averse to making suggestions, did so now.

"Emily, would you be open to a name I think the Lord wants for you?"

"Of course, Sister! I guess Sister Mary Emily isn't what you are thinking. We do have a Blessed Emily in the Order, you know."

"I know that, however, I'd like you to have Sister Maria Amata of Christ."

"You would?"

"Yes. Do you know who Blessed Amata was?"

"I recall her name coming up once, but no, I don't know who she was."

"Amata was a young woman possessed by the devil in Rome at the time of our Holy Father Saint Dominic. On one of his visits to Rome, he freed her from her possession and eventually she joined the newly reformed monastery of San Sisto. Saint Dominic gave her the name *Amata*. Do you know what the *Amata* means?"

"No. Tell me." Emily tensed in anticipation, her hands clutched tightly under her scapular.

"Emily, Saint Dominic gave her the name *Amata* because he wanted her to be assured that she was especially loved by God. I want you to have the name *Amata* because *Amata* means 'beloved.' I want you to know in a real way that you are the beloved of Christ."

Emily looked up at her novice mistress, her eyes streaming with tears. How could she express what she was feeling right now?

Sister Maria Bernadette continued. By long experience she was patient with the sisters under her care. She waited, letting the Holy Spirit do His work. She knew when the time was right to speak. This was one of those times.

"We all know that you suffered a deep loss when Dan was killed five years ago."

Emily opened her mouth to speak but the novice mistress stopped her.

"Wait. Let me finish."

"There is deep sadness and loss in your heart for your brother. You've said very little about this and have been most agreeable and cheerful with the sisters, not inflicting your occasional moods on them. Don't think I haven't noticed. Something is still troubling you...I suspect it's something about your brother. Am I right?"

Emily wordlessly nodded her head in assent.

"This is why I want you to have the name *Amata*. You are Christ's beloved. In time He will heal the deep wound in your heart if you let Him. If you are to grow in His love, to grow in holiness you must give everything—even this deep wound in your heart—to Him. Meanwhile..."

Emily interrupted.

"Please, Sister. Don't think I'm trying to keep something back that you should know. Maybe in time I'll be able to talk about this. I just can't now."

"You know I'm here if you ever need to talk. Sister Blanche Marie and Father Stephen or Father John Thomas, too. You know that?"

"Yes, I do. Thank you, Sister. It really means a lot to me. I mean that. Meanwhile, will you pray for your Sister Maria Amata?"

Sister Maria Bernadette enfolded Emily in her trademark embrace.

"Will I? I do every day. I won't stop. You'll get the graces you need. I promise. In the meantime, you better be praying for your old novice mistress!"

*   *   *

Sister Maria Amata walked hurriedly down the corridor to the nuns' choir. She was late coming in from helping Sister Catherine Cecilia with the farm chores. As she entered the ante-choir she could hear the clear resonant voice of Sister Mary Dominic intoning the first psalm. In a moment the rest of her side of choir would join in. Under the true even pitch of the sisters she would hear the sound of Sister Mary Jordan's toneless voice. Sometimes it annoyed her, but now she smiled to herself. Sister Mary Dominic and Sister Mary Jordan were long time-friends, both entering the monastery and making profession together. They had entered in the 'mid '90's, the last to enter at the old monastery. No two sisters could be more different.

"They should have named us Sister Mutt and Sister Jeff," said Sister Mary Jordan one day at recreation when Sister Maria Amata was still a new postulant. Most sisters thought that Sister Laurel and Sister Hardy would have been a more accurate label: they were known to bring the house down on big feasts when the nuns entertained each other with their home-grown "talent show."

"I mean, look at us! She sings; I croak. Well, someone has to be the frog around here. I cook—not too badly, I might add—"

"Please, Sister Mary Jordan! You overflow with humility!" This from Sister Ossana.

"Humility is truth! Isn't *Veritas* our motto? Anyway, I'll be charitable and say we're glad that Sister Mary Dominic has to put out the collation only once a week.

"I'm a chatterbox; she's a paragon of silence and recollection. What can I tell you? All I know is that we remain friends. It's all a mystery."

Sister Mary Jordan—the former Tina Hallaway—was fond of telling the story of how they had become friends.

It was at a Youth 2000 retreat way back in the early '90's.

"I looked up and saw this girl with a dirty blond Lady Di haircut—don't tell me that you don't know what *that* is; I'm not that old—sitting by herself; sort of just taking it all in. So, I walked over and said, 'You here because you want to be or because you have to.'"

"Oh, hi! Yeah, I'm here because I want to be."

She put out her hand, "Hi, my name is Anne Gallagher."

"Tina Hallaway."

She sat down next to Anne. "Where do you go to school?"

"Star of the Sea Prep. All girls. I'm a senior. What about you?"

"Me? I'm a senior, too. Public school. McCorrity High. See that girl over there with the brown curly hair talking to that Franciscan? She dragged me along—sort of. She's *really* Catholic. At the last minute a friend of hers pulled out and April didn't want to come alone. Said she was too shy! So, I said, sure. I'm Catholic—I guess. I haven't done one of these things since Confirmation retreat. In fact, I haven't gone to Mass much since. So far, this Youth 2000 thing is a lot different. Why are you here?"

"Well, it's kind of embarrassing. You won't laugh if I tell you?"

"Promise."

"SSP is all girls. Which is fine, except for one thing—"

"No guys?"

"Yep. No guys. I figured this might a good way to meet a Catholic guy. Stupid, right?"

"Well, it never crossed my mind that you'd meet someone going on a retreat! Have you been successful?"

"I've met two."

"You're kidding!"

"No, I'm not. Problem is, they're both joining the seminary next year! Can you believe it? One even suggested I might think of becoming a nun! Me! My family's devout and all that, but a nun? I'm planning to be an opera singer! What about you?"

Tina burst out laughing. It was just too funny. This conversation was nothing like McCorrity High.

"Oh, sorry—I said I wouldn't laugh! But really, why would anyone become a nun? Aren't they all old or something?"

"Yeah, that's what I thought. You know, something you do after you hit forty and your career hasn't taken off. Guess not. My school is run by nuns but none are teachers. I think there are two older ones who work in administration. They don't wear habits or anything. You have college plans or something?"

"Probably liberal arts school. Not sure if I want to major in philosophy or English. I'm not sure where I'm going yet. My dad wants me to go to a small liberal arts college in New Hampshire. Says I'll get some culture that way. They have a semester where you can study in Rome."

"Sounds cool. So what's the problem? Grades?"

"Naw, I'm on Honor Society. I'm just not sure whether I like the idea of a small college. The tuition must be wicked; and tell me, how does a liberal arts major make a living?"

"Yeah, I know what you mean. Music is no guarantee, either but at least I can sing for my supper! Come on. Why don't you hang out with me at Mass tonight? It looks like your friend April has forgotten you."

Adoration of the Blessed Sacrament that night was the beginning of a slow, steady conversion for both Tina and Anne. It was also the beginning of a deep and lasting friendship. Although they attended different colleges they kept in touch, sharing everything, except one thing. Each was afraid to share with the other a growing interest in a religious vocation. When Anne finally got up the nerve to tell Tina what she wanted to do with her life, Tina couldn't believe it. They began visiting religious communities together and both were attracted to the same monastery. The rest, as they say, was history.

*   *   *

Sister Maria Amata walked into the choir and prostrated herself full length before the prioress's stall as a penance for coming late. She waited for Sister Blanche Marie to give a quick knock with her knuckle to signal her to rise.

The novice silently made her way to her choir stall. She loved Vespers. The melodious singing quieted her and helped bring the day with all its good and bad into a small offering to the Lord. By the end of Vespers she was usually recollected for the time of private prayer before collation.

The choir was arranged the traditional way. Instead of pews facing the altar, the nuns' choir stalls ran along each side of the room facing each other. Early formation emphasized keeping one's eyes down for recollection's sake and so as not to stare at the sisters facing you on the opposite side. Tonight, though, Sister Maria Amata looked across at Sister Zita Anne.

For some reason, Sister Zita Anne often annoyed Sister Maria Amata. She wasn't sure why. They had a common bond of loss but that didn't seem to matter. Thrown together in the novitiate they were together more than with the other sisters. Sister Zita Anne, in her late '30's, exuded a deep sense of peace. She seemed content. It often rankled Sister Maria Amata.

Tonight, it was obvious Sister Zita Anne had been crying. Her pale, freckled face was red and her eyes swollen. Occasionally, she sniffled.

The nuns continued chanting the psalms:

Listen, O daughter, give ear to my words;
forget your own people and your father's house.

So the king desires your beauty;
he is your lord, pay homage to him.

Sister Maria Amata was distracted:

"Why is she crying? I wonder if Sister Mary Elaine snapped at her. She doesn't usually get upset, though. Not like I do."

The warm breeze of the June day wafted into the choir. The scent of honeysuckle was in the air. What had Sister Zita Anne told her once?

"I was married in June." Not three months later, her husband had been killed in the terrorist attack on the World Trade Center in New York. His death had tested her faith.

"I thought I could never forgive the terrorists who killed my husband. I knew I had to. It was what Jesus was calling me to do. Every day was a new effort. It took time. It took a lot of help and support from others. I was so in love! Never, and I mean never, would I have thought I'd enter a cloistered monastery. Well, here I am!"

A sudden revelation crashed into Sister Maria Amata's thoughts:

"That's what is so peaceful about her. She really forgives those guys."

Sister Mary Dominic intoned the *Magnificat*, Mary's canticle. "My soul glorifies the Lord."

Sister Maria Amata struggled to fight back the tears coming to her eyes. She looked up at the icon of Our Lady of Tenderness that was at the front of the choir.

"Mother of God and my Mother, please, help to forgive the man that killed Danny. I'm trying to, but I'm not free. Show me how to let go! Help me to be truly free, to give everything I am to God."

So with the exception of the hours which the sisters ought to consecrate to prayer,
to reading, to the preparation of the Divine Office and chant, or to study,
they should devote themselves to some manual labor, as shall be judged good by the prioress."

Constitutions of the Nuns of the Order of Preachers

CHAPTER V

Sister Maria Amata's first year as a novice went by quickly. There was another postulant in the novitiate now, Andrea, a twenty-two year old from, of all places, Australia. Her family had been in the sheep raising business for generations. Sister Andrea's dad promised the community that he would plan his annual visit to coincide with the monastery's sheep shearing season. Sister Zita Anne was now in first vows and living with the other professed sisters. Sister Maria Christi had just made solemn profession, the first to do so in the new monastery. Her profession brought her large family in two rented vans all the way from Maryland. Since the sisters had only one guestroom and since Sister Maria Christi's solemn profession took place on a beautiful day in June, the family erected a huge tent and camped out on the front expanse of property outside of the enclosure. The Bishop joked about it in his homily. "First the nuns have solar power, then they raise sheep, now they're running a summer camp! What will they do next, now that Sister Maria

Christi is a solemnly professed member of the community?"

Sister Maria Christi's profession only highlighted Sister
Maria Amata's longing for her own first profession. Her
rather distracted manner, daydreaming about it, was
quickly squelched. It was shearing season, Sister Maria
Bernadette reminded her. All hands were needed to finish
the job. Classes in the novitiate were suspended until the
work was done. Sister Blanche Marie informed Father
John Thomas that the weekly scripture classes on
Thursdays would resume in the fall.

Bill and Linda Reardon, from a sheep farm nearly two
hours away, came to shear the nuns growing flock. Bill
was getting older and slowing down. Several years ago he
had offered to teach any sisters who had the strength and
endurance how to shear. Both Sister Catherine Cecilia
and Sister Maria Christi gave it try, but they were too
slow. Sister Andrea's dad would be a welcome help. Most
likely he could get their three hundred plus flock shorn in
a couple of days.

*   *   *

Notice on the Prioress' bulletin board:

        Dear Sisters, PLEASE, everyone who can pos-
    sibly come to the weaving house loft today at
    recreation, PLEASE DO SO!!!! Fleece must be

cleaned and shipped to Vermont while the grease in them is still new. We don't want it to harden.

Get in touch with me if you can't make it. Thank you.

Written under this in Sister Mary Jordan's scribble:

Pink lemonade will be provided. Gift of the Reardons. We do not want the weary to faint along the way from lack of refreshment.

Recreation. Most of the nuns were gathered in the weaving house loft. There was just enough cross-ventilation to keep the room comfortable.

The sisters were seated on the floor, surrounded by canvas bags of fleece. It was their job to sort through them, picking out the burrs and cutting away the dirty or unusable sections. Only then could they ship this year's shearing to a co-op in Vermont. There it would be first dyed then spun into the yarn that would become their hand-woven blankets.

As usual when the community was gathered for projects like this, the atmosphere was joyful, almost playful. Sister Mary Dominic and Sister Mary Jordan were keeping up a lively exchange of pithy remarks.

"OK. Is anyone beginning to wonder if maybe, just maybe, they might have been more useful to the Church and society if they had stayed out in 'the world?'"

Sister Mary Jordan threw a section of fleece matted with dried excrement in the general direction of Sister Mary Dominic.

"And why, pray tell, should you be asking us that question? Could it be you're finding this job not to your liking?"

Sister Mary Jordan threw a burr back at her friend.

"You have to admit, we *are* a bit over-qualified for this job! I mean look at us! A bunch of college-educated women cleaning out sheep fleece!"

There was laughter.

"Can you imagine what *Vogue* would think if they saw Sister Regina now!" said Sister Maria Christine.

Sister Regina was wearing her oldest most discolored work habit. Her veil was patched and her Nike sneakers had holes.

"I hardly think that being a model was any great contribution to society. Besides, look at me: do you really think I'd be doing much modeling at fifty-seven?"

"Maybe you'd be doing Vioxx ads" said Sister Maria Amata. "You know: 'After thirty-five years of modeling my smile has arthritis. With Vioxx I can continue smiling all day!'"

Sister Regina threw a piece of dirty fleece at her: "You guys are nuts! What about the other sisters?"

Sister Mary Dominic placed a stray piece of hay in her mouth, sucked on it and squinted at Sister Blanche Marie.

"How 'bout you, Sister Blanche? What do you think you'd be doing?"

"Maybe I'd still be in the Army, but I doubt it. One thing is certain, I wouldn't be translating for the Holy Father!"

A polyglot, Sister Blanche could speak and read five languages with ease. Before entering the monastery she had been a translator in the Army.

"I know one thing," stated Sister Mary Dominic. "Sister Maria Christine would probably be in textiles. Hey, maybe she'd be designing strange-looking outfits for Sister Regina to model!"

"Or maybe you'd be wearing them giving concerts. Sometimes *divas* wear strange looking things!"

"Well, maybe *you'd* be wearing a frumpy-looking suit teaching in a high school!"

"Hey, knock it off! I seem to remember that *you* didn't have the most fashionable haircut when we first met!"

"Please, sisters, enough!" pleaded Sister Blanche Marie.

Sister Mary Elaine decided to change the subject.

"Why don't you tell the sisters what you were talking to Father John Thomas about this morning?"

"Don't tell us the Holy Father has another book for us to produce?" whined Sister Mary Dominic. She was Sister Blanche Marie's assistant.

"No. To be honest I think I'd tell him, 'With all due respect, Holy Father, right now is not a good time for a

book. We have all we can handle getting next year's line of
blankets underway.'"

Sister Blanche *could* speak to the Pope frankly. After
all, she had known him since he was a student brother.

"By the way, Sister Mary Elaine, how is your translation coming along? Almost finished?"

Sister Mary Elaine was Russian on her mother's side.
She spoke it fluently. The Pope always said that Sister
Mary Elaine could really catch his ideas in between the
lines and get them right.

"It's coming; but I tell you, sometimes he isn't easy to
translate—into English, I mean! I've had to get in touch
with him a few times to clarify things." She let out a long
sigh: "His secretary doesn't always make it easy for me."

Sister Maria Christine interrupted: "Would you two
stop talking shop. What were you going to tell us, Sister
Blanche Marie?"

"I was going to wait and share this with you at chapter
tomorrow, but since Sister Mary Elaine has spilled the
beans—

"I was talking with Father John Thomas this morning.
He says that a church in New York is being closed by the
Archdiocese." She paused waiting to have the full atten-
tion of the sisters. "He says it has an old Italian bell. The
tone is beautiful. He thinks they might give it to us if we
provide the transportation."

"Whoopee! A real bell! A real monastery!" Sister Catherine Cecilia threw a piece of dirty fleece in the air. She watched it land on top of Sister Regina's head.

Sister Catherine Cecilia scrambled up off the floor and went over to Sister Regina.

"Please, dear Sister. I'm so sorry. I didn't mean a single piece of my darlings' fleece to land on your head. Bend down; let me clean the dung off your 'do!"

Sister Andrea doubled over laughing. This community was nothing like her mental picture of cloistered nuns. It was great.

Sister Maria Bernadette caught sight of Sister Maria Amata silently bent over her pile of fleece. She looked angry; she was trying not to cry.

"I wonder what *that's* all about? She said to herself. "You'd think she'd be happy that we'll have a bell tower. I wonder if this has something to do with her brother. I'll have to keep my eye on her."

Meanwhile, Sister Mary Dominic and Sister Maria Christi had stood up and grabbed Sister Mary Jordan's hands. The three of them began circling the group on the floor. They began singing: "Ding, dong, merrily on high, in heav'n the bells are ringing." Sister Maria Christi began kicking, encouraging the others into a fake can-can.

"Sisters, please! What *are* you doing?"

"Goofing off. Remember the scene in 'The Grinch that Stole Christmas?' All the *Whos* of *Who-ville* dancing around the Christmas tree in the town square."

"Sorry. That's after my time," responded Sister Blanche Marie, acknowledging that what they were referring to took place *after* her entrance into the monastery.

She sighed. "I knew I should have waited 'til chapter tomorrow to give you the news!"

Our communion embraces with special concern nuns who are undergoing difficulties.

Constitutions of the Nuns of the Order of Preachers

CHAPTER VI

Bang.

Bang. Swish.

Bang.

Sister Ossana walked passed the closed door of the laundry and paused. Who was making that racket? She backtracked and opened the door. There she saw Sister Maria Amata at the sink.

Sister Maria Amata looked up.

"Oh, hi. I'm sorry; was I making too much noise?" she asked dully. Her tone of voice expressed that she really didn't care if she was.

She was scrubbing her habit in the sink. Wearing white, especially on a sheep farm, meant lots of stains. Scrubbing the habits before throwing them in the washing machine was a necessity if the sisters were going to keep their habits looking presentable.

"Well, let's say that what I heard coming from in here wasn't the soundtrack of the Sound of Music."

"Sorry."

It was after collation. Strictly it was silence time but Sister Ossana sensed that something was going on with Sister Maria Amata.

"Aren't you usually putting the farm to bed at this time?"

"Yeah, usually. Sister Andrea is doing it on Thursdays so that I can get my habit scrubbed before tomorrow's wash."

Sister Ossana decided to change the subject.

"Oh, hey, I wasn't at recreation this afternoon; too many bills to catch up on in the bursar's office. Sister Blanche Marie told me the great news about the bell. Of course we'll have to vote on it in chapter but—"

"It is NOT great news!"

Sister Maria Amata flung down the brown soap she held in her hand slamming it into the sink. It flew into the air hitting Sister Ossana.

"Oh! Oh! Oh, Sister, I'm sorry! I didn't mean that! Are you OK?"

The tears began pouring down her cheeks.

Sister Ossana was stunned. "What is this all about, Sister Maria Amata? What's the matter?"

She dimly remembered that she was out of bounds asking that question. She really should get Sister Maria Bernadette. Right now, she thought, that wasn't a good idea. She continued:

"Sister, what are you so angry about? What's wrong? Did I do something to you? Did I say something? If I did, I'm truly sorry."

Sister Maria Amata stood limply before Sister Ossana, sobbing.

"Sister, no, it's not you. I'm so sorry. It's NOT great news! It's NOT!"

"Is this all about the bell? What's so awful about our getting a bell?"

"You don't understand. No one here understands—"

Sister Ossana grasped Sister Maria Amata by her arms, forcing her to stand directly in front of her.

"Sister, look at me."

Sister Maria Amata looked up.

"You're right. I don't understand what this is all about. All I know is that you're very upset about our getting the bell, and that it has some awful meaning for you. You have to help me. Can't you tell me?"

"Danny…my brother…" Sniff. "The one that got killed at the seminary."

"What about him? What does he have to do with our getting a bell?"

Sister Maria Amata took a deep breath, and then let out a long audible sigh.

"Danny was the bell ringer for the seminary.... It was a Saturday afternoon in late fall. The seminarians were out raking the leaves on the front lawn.... Danny was one of them.... Suddenly out of nowhere, a guy is in front of them and starts shooting at them, just shooting in all directions. He was crazy. He had to have been.... Danny started running toward the bell tower and began ringing the bell, trying to call for help. One of Danny's friends who was shot said that the sound of the bell seemed to infuriate the man even more. He turned and began walking toward Danny, his gun pointed straight at him....Danny was so busy pulling the rope he never even noticed....Suddenly the man pointed directly at Danny and shot him. He died instantly. And then the man shot himself."

Sister Ossana pulled the sobbing novice toward her. Amata flung her face on Sister Ossana's shoulder and continued to sob.

"It's OK, dear. Keep crying. Keep crying. You need to get this out." She attempted to soothe the sobbing novice. "It's OK; it's OK."

"Danny and I were so close....We would be partners....He'd say to me, 'Emi, I'll do the preaching and you'll do the praying.' I've tried to forgive the man who killed Danny. I AM trying. Everyday it's an effort. I'm waiting for the grace. I have to let go.... I just miss Dan so much."

Several minutes later Sister Maria Amata raised her head from the sub-prioress's shoulder and faced her. The tears were still flowing from her eyes but she was no longer angry.

"Thank you, sister. Thanks. She fumbled in her pocket for a handkerchief, coming up short. "Darn it all, where's my hanky?"

Sister Ossana turned toward a basket of laundry. She rummaged through it, finally pulling out an old worn piece of cloth.

"Here. I think this is supposed to be a hanky. I think it's clean. It's better than nothing.

"Here. Blow your nose."

Sister Maria Amata took it shyly from the sub-prioress. She spoke hesitantly.

"I suppose...I suppose you'll have to tell Sister Maria Bernadette about this outburst of mine?"

"I guess so. 'Course, it would be a good idea if you told her yourself. Will you?"

"Yeah. I guess I have to. She doesn't know any of this, either. I couldn't talk about it. I guess I needed to...."

"I guess you did. Look. It's almost time for Compline. Are you OK?"

"Yeah, I'm fine. Thanks again for putting up with me. Thanks for being here for me."

"You bet. What are sisters for!" She smiled.

When you come to serve the Lord, prepare yourself for trials.

Sirach 2:1-5

Chapter VII

"…Naturally, we are all happy about the possibility of obtaining a bell for our monastery. God in His loving Providence has provided us with the necessities to make our life possible all along. We know in His goodness that sometimes He also likes to provide us with things that are not strictly necessary. You might say we're spoiled."

It was the regular Friday afternoon chapter meeting. The community was assembled in the chapter hall seated on benches along each side of the narrow room facing each other as in the choir. Only the prioress and sub-prioress sat at the top of the room beneath the large crucifix facing the nuns. On either side of the crucifix were hand-carved images of Our Lady and Saint Dominic. Sister Blanche Marie continued:

"But in the history of the Church and in our monastic tradition, a bell is more than an object that is pleasant to the ear. It has a symbolic significance. The bell is the voice of God calling us to prayer. It is also a reminder to the people who live around us of the priority of prayer, both in our lives and in theirs.

"Some of you may know that church bells are consecrated. Usually they are blessed and anointed by the Bishop. Only then can they be used. Consecrated bells are often described as being baptized. This is so, because so many features of the ceremonial of the inauguration of bells is similar to the rite of Baptism. The bell is even given a name! Hopefully by next week I will learn the name of the bell being offered to us and share this with you.

"Because this bell has already been consecrated we will not have such a ceremony. Perhaps we will have a little ceremony the day we begin using the bell. I'd ask Sister Mary Dominic, since she is liturgy director, to investigate an appropriate format of prayers, etc. Also, Sister, if you could go the library and pull out the rite of consecration for bells and leave it in the library for the sisters to read, I'd appreciate it.

"There will be no discussion after proclamation of faults today. We will have a chapter discussion next week regarding this topic. Acquiring this bell will mean a significant outlay. We also need to decide where we want to build the tower should we vote to accept this offer. Matty has some ideas. I can present them next week."

Matty Reilly was their handyman and jack-of-all-trades. "What would we do without Matty?" was Sister Blanche's repeated exclamation. The other nuns felt the same. Matty loved the nuns and considered his job with them his vocation. In his youth he had entered the Dominican Order as a cooperator brother but left before solemn vows. No one knew why. "Had to study too much theology," was Matty's complaint, but friars who knew him said he was a good student and that there must have been other reasons. Shortly after Mater Christi Monastery was founded, Matty had gone to the Provincial asking if he knew where he might find a job. The Provincial knew the nuns were looking for a handyman and suggested the job to Matty. For Matty it was a dream come true. Unknown to the nuns he had made a private vow to remain at the monastery as long as they wanted him.

Matty lived in the Chaplain's house and provided companionship and male camaraderie in a predominantly female atmosphere. He would attend Lauds, Mass and Vespers in the extern part of the chapel and was often seen there in solitary prayer. He loved the silence of the monastery yet he was not averse to engaging in a heated theological discussion with either Father Stephen or Father John Thomas into the late hours of the evening.

Sister Blanche Marie concluded her announcements:

"Next Friday I would ask that Sister Zita Anne prepare Collation. Sister Maria Amata and Sister Andrea, if you would do the farm chores so that the chapter nuns can be free for an extended discussion—there are several items on the agenda—I'd be grateful."

Inwardly, Sister Mary Jordan groaned:

"Oh great, an extended discussion. There goes the afternoon!"

"We will now proceed with the proclamation of faults."

Chapter of faults was an ancient monastic custom. In order to grow in self-knowledge and to encourage each other, the sisters confessed not sins—that was not permitted—but external faults against the rule and constitutions and the customs of the monastery. Accusing another sister was never allowed. To newcomers the practice seemed outdated and neurotic. For the nuns, chapter of faults was a way of asking pardon of the community. It also helped to know that others struggled with the same things.

The prioress rose at her place and began: "Sisters, I accuse myself of being careless and leaving my mops and brooms at the door for someone else to shake out. Whichever kind sister took care of them, I thank you and ask pardon for my carelessness." She sat down.

Each nun rose spontaneously to proclaim her faults if she felt inclined. Most did.

"I accuse myself of purposely being late for choir."

"I accuse myself of not keeping the silence and chatting out at the sheep barn without necessity."

"I accuse myself...."

"I accuse myself of letting the soup for collation burn. Sisters, I ask your forgiveness. I know I've done this several times," said Sister Mary Dominic. A few nuns smiled.

"I accuse myself...."

Sister Maria Amata waited for the professed nuns to finish before she would speak. Sister Maria Bernadette told her that in the old days the novices proclaimed their faults first then left the room. The nuns of Mater Christi figured that since the novices interacted with the professed nuns so much they might as well be a part of the chapter like everyone else. Sister Andrea was not permitted to attend as a postulant.

"Sisters, I accuse myself of creating a scene and a disturbance in the laundry last night. I also accuse myself of rude and angry behavior toward another sister." She glanced up at Sister Ossana. "I ask her forgiveness." She sat down.

Sister Blanche concluded the short ceremony.

"If there is nothing else, I will now assign the penance. Sisters, today I ask that you each pray three Hail Mary's for someone especially in need of our prayers."

Sister Maria Amata had had a long talk with her novice mistress that morning telling her everything about her brother's death and her own struggle to forgive. Later, Sister Maria Bernadette had shared the gist of the conversation with Sister Blanche Marie:

"From what she tells me, she has struggled with many emotions about her brother's death but kept a lot of it under wraps because of her parents. She said it was devastating for them, especially for her dad. He just can't understand why God would permit such a violent thing to happen to a young man who was dedicating his life to the priesthood. She didn't want to add to their grief by expressing how she felt. Of course, once she got here and began living our intense inner life she just couldn't hold it in much longer. Your announcing the news about the bell was the last straw."

"Poor Sister Maria Amata! Both she and Sister Zita Anne have had incredible personal sorrow at such an early age. It's hard to imagine what they have had to deal with."

The prioress paused then looked up at the Crucifix on the wall.

"You know, God must love them very much to ask them to share in His Son's Passion this way."

"I know. That's what I've always thought. That's why I wanted Sister Maria Amata to have the name *Amata*—it means beloved."

Sister Blanche Marie hesitated. "I hate to ask this question, but I suppose I must. Do you think Sister Maria Amata is emotionally stable enough for our life? She has to come to terms with this anger she struggles with, or she will be a disturbance to the community. Sister Ossana said that the outburst in the laundry was quite intense."

"Sister Blanche, yes, I think that on the whole she is emotionally stable. I think she has a true vocation. She tells me that she has often talked to Father Stephen about this in Confession and spiritual direction, and that she is waiting for the grace to totally let go of her anger toward the man who killed Danny—to be free. She says that before she entered the monastery she couldn't even pray for his salvation but now she does everyday. His name was Adam Kensel. No one knows anything about him. I guess he was a real loner.

"I believe her. It may take time, but just sharing this with us is a great grace. We have to give God room to work in her. We have to be patient."

"Good. I like Sister Maria Amata a lot. She seems to fit in with our community. I'd hate to lose her."

"I would, too. She's a good sister in so many ways. She's generous. She doesn't particularly like working with Sister Mary Elaine, but I know that ever since she learned Sister hurt her back she sneaks down to the barn to fill the water buckets for her. I've noticed that lately she is more friendly and outgoing with Sister Zita Anne. At first she was like an icicle with her. She's starting to warm up. I think she's not trying so hard to be accepted."

"You know, Sister," responded the prioress, "the longer I'm in the monastery the more I marvel at the mystery of a vocation. Over and over I see women come, enthused to give everything to God, to become saints and to save souls. Nothing will stand in their way. Then they enter the monastery and, bang-o!—They are faced with their own weaknesses, frailties and sins. And they don't like it! They want to deny it, make it go away but they must face their frailty—they must face that they are part of the human race. Not only that, they have to realize and accept that only by God's grace is any of this life possible."

Sister Maria Bernadette responded: "I know. In novice after novice I see the same pattern, yet in each one the struggle, the fight, and most of all the surrender to God's love, is different. He treats each sister so uniquely. I'm always amazed. I've noticed it's the more devout ones that have the hardest time. I don't mean to say that they enter with an attitude, but they're the ones who have the hardest time accepting that the rest of us are not walking around with little notebooks recording their words and actions for a future canonization process!

"It's so beautiful to watch them as they grow in prayer, and in self-knowledge. They gradually respond to the graces that God is giving them. It's really a privilege to be a part of it. I just pray daily that I don't interfere and mess up what God wants to do in their lives."

"Don't I know it," interjected Sister Blanche Marie. "Every morning that's my prayer: 'Lord Jesus Christ, Son of God, help me to lead this community in Your Truth.' Frankly, I'll be happy for the day when my term of office runs out. I don't know how much purgatory time I've accumulated in the past four years!"

"We must pray for one another and trust that God will bring something out of our mistakes!"

Sister Maria Bernadette stopped and listened. Faintly, in the distance she could here the clang of the hand bell calling the sisters to the Rosary.

"And I know one thing! I'll be one happy nun when we finally have a bell I can hear!"

Thy face, Lord, do I seek. Hide not thy face from me
Psalm 27

CHAPTER VIII

Shortly after her conversation with the prioress, Sister Maria Bernadette asked Sister Maria Amata if she would like a few days in solitude, alone only with God...and her thoughts.

"If you want to you may go up to the hermitage for three days. Sister Blanche Marie thought you might need the time and quiet."

She was thrilled. Matty and the nuns had built a hermitage in a clearing on the edge of the woods using stones from an old stone wall. It was about as primitive as you could get. It was little more than a hut with a dirt floor, a door and one window. Nearby was a spring where the sisters could get water. As a concession to modern life they curtained off an alcove and installed a portable toilet. In another corner they hung a large crucifix and icon of Our Lady. Below it was a shelf with the Scriptures lovingly placed. There was a sleeping bag rolled up in another corner and an ancient rocking chair. There was no heat and no electricity.

The nuns loved their hermitage, which they named *Maria Silencii*, Mary of the Silence. They often went up there for their monthly personal retreat day. Only with special permission from Sister Blanche Marie could they sleep there overnight. Before Sister Maria Christi's solemn profession, she had spent her entire retreat at the hermitage, coming down to the monastery only for Mass and provisions. On the first day Father John Thomas led the entire community up carrying the Blessed Sacrament, which would remain in the hermitage for the ten days. When they got to the hermitage the community prayed a special litany of the saints. Then Father John Thomas blessed the hermitage with the Blessed Sacrament and everyone left. When Sister Maria Christi returned to the community at Vespers the day before her profession, she was radiant. Sister Mary Elaine thought of Moses coming down the mountain after forty days with God.

Sister Maria Bernadette told the novice that she was only required to attend Mass and Vespers. "After Vespers, wait for me at the side vestibule door." She was concerned that the total solitude not be too extreme for her young novice. Each evening she would decide if Sister Maria Amata should be permitted to spend the night in the hermitage.

After Mass on the second day, Sister Maria Amata went to the boot room off the kitchen to pick up the bread, cheese and fruit that Sister Mary Jordan would pack for her day's meal. Wrapped around a large piece of dark chocolate was the following note:

+

Dear Sister MA,

The rule of Saint Augustine says that we should eat whatever is put before us so I hope you'll eat this piece of chocolate. Sister Ossana found it in the top drawer of her desk and remembered that you love dark chocolate, too. Enjoy.

Yesterday, Sister B called a chapter to tell us about Danny and why you are on retreat in the her-mitage. Sister, I'm sorry about Danny. We didn't know. I will pray for him and the man who killed him everyday.

I will pray for you, too. Please pray for me while you are hiding under God's wings. Oh, by the way, if you see any wild flowers that I might want to press, pick them for me. Thanks.

May the Virgin and her Child bless you.

Your sister,

SMJ

Sister Maria Amata smiled through her tears. Good ol' Sister Mary Jordan! She would have to remember to thank Sister Ossana for the chocolate. Chocolate was a rare treat. The sisters said that at the old monastery they received so much chocolate from friends and benefactors that they would often give part of it away to the poor. Now, people didn't have the money to give such treats to the nuns. Father Stephen had taken to giving each nun a chocolate bar on her feast day. He knew who liked milk chocolate and who liked dark. Sister Ossana was probably giving Sister Maria Amata her feast day treat.

Sister Maria Amata spent her days in solitude roaming the hills and woods. Her father had taught her to sing the rosary and she would sing it as she walked. She could hear the bleating of the ewes in the lower pasture. She would make her way to the large flat boulder in the middle of the upper field, sit on it cross-legged and pray her breviary, singing the psalms out loud. The local people said that it was the tombstone of an Indian princess. Sister Maria Amata didn't doubt it.

The monastery seemed a million miles away although sometimes she could hear Matty shouting instructions to Sister Catherine Cecilia. Sister Maria Amata found her first night in the hermitage a scary experience. She could hear the crunching of deer hooves on the pine needles in the silence. Surrounded by the wind in the trees and the wildlife in the woods, she felt watched by unseen eyes. Before going to sleep she blessed the hermitage with holy water, flinging it about the room in the form of a large cross. She unrolled the sleeping bag under the crucifix and, fully dressed in her habit, crawled into it, her rosary and crucifix in her hand. In five minutes she was fast asleep.

*   *   *

It was an early September morning. Sister Maria Amata was busy with Sister Maria Christine and Sister Zita Anne in the weaving house. There was no doubt about it; orders were coming in more quickly lately. There was even talk of purchasing another loom. Sister Maria Amata hoped that wouldn't happen. She didn't want to see their cottage industry become too big and start to take over their contemplative lives. She could see the news head-lines: "Monastery closes amid conflict over the success of 'Golden Run Blankets.' Nuns tied up in knots!"

"The devil would really like that, he really would," mused Sister Maria Amata.

Swish. Whamp, whamp.

Swish. Whamp, whamp.

Sister Maria Amata's body moved to the rhythm of the weaving. She loved weaving. Usually the even beat and dance with her feet on the shaft pedals recollected her and led her to pray. She understood why weavers often sang as they wove.

Today, however, she was tense. If she looked out the windows of the weaving house she could see Matty and another man pouring the concrete for the bell tower platform. Along side it on a piece of tarp, sat the new bell gleaming in the sunshine.

When Matty heard about the bell, he called up Father Provincial and made his request:

"Father Provincial, I need a favor." Matty and Father Joseph had been classmates long ago when Matty was still a novice but he always called the provincial, 'Father Provincial.'

"Listen. Did ya hear about the nuns getting a bell?....You did. OK. So how do you think they're going to get it out here?...You have no idea....Well, I have an idea. It's the end of the summer, right? The student brothers haven't returned to the House of Studies from their summer ministry yet, have they?...Well, how about they do a little 'ministry' for their sisters...Yeah, I'm not kidding. You've got five strong, young brothers in New York, right? How 'bout you let me have them for the week. We'll load the bell on a truck, bring it out here and build the tower...Yes, we can do it in a week. What do you think I'm building, a bell tower for Ravenna? The nuns don't have money for anything but a basic steel structure...I promise. You'll have the brothers back in a week.... Thanks. I appreciate it. The nuns will be so grateful they'll probably weave you a blanket."

Swish. Whamp. Whamp.

Sister Maria Amata found herself weaving to the rhythm of the men hammering the steel.

Cling. Cling.

Swish. Whamp. Whamp.

Cling. Cling.

She wished she could block out the sound but she couldn't. She began talking to herself:

"Soon there will be a tower, then a bell, then—"

Sister Maria Amata stopped weaving and leaned her forehead against the breast beam of the loom.

"Oh, no! Oh, I hope not! She wouldn't do that to me, would she? O sweet Jesus, help me!"

If there is a bell then *someone* will have to ring it!

Every Mass.

Every Office.

Every Angelus.

Every day.

Sister Maria Amata could feel the sweat pouring down her back and under her veil. Didn't Sister Mary Elaine tell her once that it was traditional that the oldest novice ring the bell?

"Lord Jesus, Son of God, have mercy on me a sinner!"

Perhaps Sister Blanche Marie wouldn't do that. Perhaps she'd ask for volunteers. She wouldn't have to offer. No one would have to know how she dreaded to touch that rope. Maybe—

A little voice inside Sister Maria Amata spoke:

"Stop running. You can't run away from this. You MUST ring that bell!"

"NO! NO! I don't have to offer! I don't, I don't!"

"So, are you going to spend your whole life running? What did you come here for? Do you really want what God wants? Or do you just want your own way?"

Sister Maria Amata's eyes filled with tears. She struggled not to cry. She didn't want the other sisters seeing her. They'd ask what was wrong. Then she'd lie. She was too ashamed to tell the truth.

Sister Maria Amata got up from her loom and walked over to the door. She stood in the doorway, her arms folded under her scapular, allowing her eyes to adjust to the sunlight. Quietly she watched Matty and two of the student brothers working. Her right hand found the rosary hanging from her side and she began praying, fingering the worn cocoa beads. Why had she *really* come to the monastery? Was she running? Was she willing to go all the way?

"Lord," she whispered softly, "open my heart to You. I don't want to turn back now."

The men continued hammering. Behind her Sister Maria Amata could hear the sisters weaving. There was no wind and the cicadas in the trees were screeching their finale of the season. Vaguely, Sister Maria Amata remembered a short poem she had read from a book by Jan Karon at the beach while still in college. What was the first line?

Ring the bells....How did it go? She remembered being struck by the last line. It was so long ago—before Danny....

Ring the bells that still can ring,
Forget your perfect offering.
There is a crack in everything
That's how the light gets in.

Forget your perfect offering, Emily. *There is a crack in everything.* Boy, do you have a crack! A biggie and you don't want anyone seeing it. Heaven forbid that you should be imperfect like everyone else. Are you going to let the Light in or not? Forget your perfect offering.

Ring the bells that still can ring...that's how the light gets in.

What you long for will be given to you.
What you desire will be yours forever.

St. Leo the Great, Homily 65

CHAPTER IX

Sister Blanche posted a sign on the bulletin board:

Chapter after None.
Blessing of the sisters appointed to the Office of Bell
Ringer.

It was September 13th. Matty and the brothers had finished the bell tower in a week as promised. A few days ago
the brothers had hung the bell in the tower and left the
monastery in high spirits. Having the brothers for an
entire week had been a wonderful experience for the community. Sister Mary Elaine had even cajoled them into
doing some of the heavy work around the barn. The
brothers stay meant extra work for the kitchen and the
laundry, but the nuns didn't mind. As for the brothers,
their view of the life of their contemplative nuns changed
forever!

Sister Blanche Marie decided that the community would inaugurate the use of the bell on September 14th, feast of the Exaltation of the Holy Cross. Not only was it a beautiful feast but it was also the day when the community began their traditional monastic fast until Easter. It was a fitting day to begin ringing their new bell.

The ceremony at chapter was simple. Once the sisters had gathered Sister Blanche Marie filled the community in on the new procedures:

"I've asked Sister Maria Christi, Sister Zita Anne and Sister Maria Amata to serve as Bell Ringers for the rest of my term of office as Prioress. Sr Maria Christi will ring for Mass, Sister Zita Anne will ring for the Offices and Sister Maria Amata will ring the *Angelus* at six in the morning before Lauds, noon after Sext and six in the evening before collation. We will continue to use the hand bell for Matins. We don't need to wake our neighbors *that* early in the morning.

"I know some of you have been worried about the reaction of our neighbors concerning the bell. On his trips to town Matty has been telling people, eliciting their reaction. Most have been quite positive. One man told Matty that it will be a good way for him not to forget God in his life. A woman at the post office said that the bell will be a reminder to her of our role in the community. She might even remember to drop off some eggs.

"Now, if Sister Maria Christi, Sister Zita Anne and Sister Maria Amata would come forward and prostrate I will bless you with holy water."

*   *   *

That morning Sister Maria Bernadette had called Sister Maria Amata into her office.

"Sister, I know you may not be happy to hear this, but Sister Blanche Marie asked me if I thought you would be able to manage ringing the *Angelus* bell."

Sister Maria Amata tensed. Surely the novice mistress had told the prioress that she couldn't do it!

"I told her 'yes.'" She waited.

"Did you have to? I mean, couldn't you have let me off?"

"No. Sister Maria Amata, as difficult as this is for you, you *can* do this! You know that. You can't let an irrational fear like this get in the way of community life. It's part of maturing; of doing your part in the community. Can you imagine if Sister Mary Dominic refused to serve as chantress every time she's had a bad day? Or if Sister Mary Elaine decided that she's had enough of sheep and decided to take a few days off without telling anyone?

"In a few months you will be eligible for first profession of vows. By allowing you to make profession, the community is saying that they believe you are ready to make this commitment of total surrender to God and that you are ready to assume your part in the responsibility we all share to make this community work with God's help.

"Are you willing to be one of the bell ringers? I'm not forcing you. You must choose freely. You must obey freely."

Sister Maria Amata sat still for more than a few minutes. *I'm not forcing you. You must choose freely. You must obey freely.* The words of the novice mistress echoed in her mind. She looked up at Sister Maria Bernadette. In a voice barely louder than a whisper she said,

"I accept. I don't know how I'm going to do it but I obey with all my heart." She smiled. "I just hope you're praying for me!"

*   *   *

No matter how much Sister Maria Amata wanted to obey, once she heard the Prioress call her name she froze to her seat. *I can't! I can't!*

Sister Andrea nudged her arm and whispered: "Sister Maria Amata, move. Sister Blanche Marie is calling you!"

Sister Maria Amata slowly got up. Her legs felt like jelly. *I can't! I can't!*

"YOU CAN!" another voice inside her said.

Sister Maria Amata knelt alongside the other two sisters, kissed her scapular and dropped to the floor, her forehead leaning against her folded arms. Far away she could hear Sister Blanche Marie's voice: "May the Lord bring this good work He has begun in you to completion.

In the name of the Father, and of the Son and of the Holy Spirit. Sisters, you may rise. May the Lord reward you for your service to the community."

*   *   *

Sister Maria Amata rose from her place in choir after Sister Mary Elaine read the scripture reading and walked to the side door. Sister Maria Bernadette had given her instructions before the Office:

"During the silence after the reading go out to the bell. Begin ringing when you hear the fire horn from town announcing the noon hour."

Sister Maria Amata walked out the door into the September sunlight. She carefully closed the door behind her and stood looking up at the bell hanging in the tower standing at the edge of the clearing between the choir and the weaving house. *Antonio.* Long ago the bell had been baptized *Antonio.* St. Anthony, patron of lost articles. *Will he help me find forgiveness and peace?*

There was a slight wind. There was silence in the trees.

Sister Maria Amata wished Matty wasn't in town today. He'd ring the bell for her if she asked. No one would have to know. She could hear Sister Zita Anne sing the closing response. In a few seconds, Sister Catherine Cecilia would chant the closing prayer. Then—

She squinted, looking at the bell hanging up there so innocently. The sweat began pouring down her back. Sister Maria Amata began walking toward the bell tower.

She could feel the dry field grass crunching under her sandals. The bell wasn't so far away as this, was it? Sister Maria Amata looked ahead and tried to focus despite the black spots before her eyes.

Great! I'll faint! I don't want to have to explain that one to Sister Maria Bernadette!

Sister Maria Amata looked at her watch. In less then a minute, if it was accurate, the fire horn would begin to blow. She approached the tower platform and stood still. The rope hanging from the bell made her think of a gibbet. What had Sister Mary Elaine threatened:

"Next spring I'll plant marigolds around the bell platform!"

"You wouldn't dare!" Sister Mary Jordan had said. "Yuck, they stink!"

Sister Maria Amata stood directly in front of the rope. Slowly she encircled her hands around it her fists resting on the knots Matty had made to help the nuns grip the rope more firmly. She could feel the scratchy roughness of the thick plaited rope.

The novice heard a noise behind her and wheeled around. Wasn't that a man she saw at the edge of the woods?

She took a deep breath. *That isn't a man, you cracked nut! That's a deer!*

Sister Blanche Marie had told her that the *Angelus* consisted of three groups of three tolls of the bell, rung slowly with pauses between each one, and a longer hold between each group. Then the bell should swing twelve to fifteen times. She doubted she'd be able to endure through it.

The fire horn blared in the distance.

Sister Maria Amata grabbed the rope and pulled weakly.

Bong

The Angel of the Lord declared unto Mary.

She gripped the rope in her sweating hands and squatted down to the ground, her heels bracing her to sustain the silence between each toll.

Sister Maria Amata could hear Danny's voice:

"Emi, that's pathetic! You call that ringing the bell?"

She released her grip slightly, allowing the swing of the bell to pull her up off the ground, off her heels and onto her toes.

Bong

Ring the bells that still can ring....you must choose freely.... you must obey freely.

BONG

What did you come here for?...you must give it all to God....even the deep wound in your heart. You must forgive.

BONG

Amata, do you love me?...Lord, you know that I love you.

BONG

Since God so loved us, we also ought to love one another...Amata, beloved of Christ.

BONG

There is a crack in everything...that is how the light gets in.

BONG

I am the light of the world...Let go of your anger, Amata. Don't hold anything from Me.

BONG

Only when you surrender it all to Him will you be truly free.

BONG

Sister Maria Amata held the bell still one more time before releasing it for the final peal. Again she let the force of the wheel lift her off her heels and onto her toes, shooting her body up like an arrow. It was freeing. She could feel the strain of her fears release and vanish into the air as the sound of the bell echoed.

She tolled the last peal with joy in her heart, enjoying the feel of the bell. Each swing of the bell lifted the heavy burden in her heart. She would hold nothing back. It was all His. She would forgive the man who killed Danny and the other seminarians. Didn't God love him, too? Hadn't she come here to offer her life for the salvation of souls?

Flushed, perspiring and happy, Sister Maria Amata turned away from the bell rope and began walking toward the monastery. Her veil had slid back and wisps of hair were escaping all over her face. She looked up and saw Sister Maria Bernadette standing at the doorway watching her. Sister Maria Amata stopped in front of the novice mistress.

"I rang the *Angelus* bell."

"So I heard."

She smiled. She took Sister Maria Amata's hand with one hand and with the other began pushing the wisps of hair back under her veil.

"Come into the house and get some dinner. I hear Sister Mary Jordan is serving bean stew."

Sister Maria Bernadette put her arm around Sister Maria Amata and led her into the house. It was bright, austere and welcoming. It was peaceful; a place of prayer.

It was home.

THE END

GLOSSARY OF TERMS

Lectio Divina or "Holy Reading" is a slow, careful reading of Sacred Scripture allowing God to speak to us through His Word. "We speak to God when we pray, we hear Him when we read the divine sayings." (Saint Ambrose) *Lectio Divina* is a preparation for the gift of Contemplation.

Divine Office or Liturgy of the Hours which consists of hymns, psalms, readings from Scripture and writings of the Church Fathers and the Saints is the official prayer of the Church. While monastic men and women are deputed by the Church to this work of divine praise, all the baptized are encourage to pray the Divine Office.

Matins, Lauds, Vespers, Compline are the "hours" of the Divine Office. While called "hours" each Office, in fact, takes about a half hour or less to chant. The so-called "Little Hours" of **Terce, Sext** and **None** are shorter and take only about ten minutes. Seven times each day the nuns lay aside their work to pray, thereby sanctifying the whole day.

Postulant, Novice, First Profession are the stages in formation toward the complete consecration of solemn vows, which consecrate the nun permanently until death. It takes approximately seven years of study and formation before solemn vows. The first stage, *Postulancy*, (from the Latin word meaning "to ask") is the initial stage when the young woman merely lives with the community, observing and being observed by the nuns. After about a year if she should be found suitable, the nuns vote and accept the Postulant into the *Noviciate*. She receives the habit of the Order, and a religious name which may be her baptized name or a new one. After two years the nuns vote again to allow the novice to make *First Profession* which is the temporary commitment made for three years before the definitive commitment of *Solemn Profession*. During the time of Noviciate, the sister may freely leave or be asked to leave. During the time of First Vows, she must obtain the permission of the Bishop. Requests for departure by a solemnly professed nun are reserved to the Pope.

The chapter is the official body of Solemnly Professed nuns under the presidency of the Prioress which has the competency to examine and decide matters of major importance for the community according to the rule and constitutions.

Chapter of Faults or **Regular Chapter** is when the monastic community gathers to examine itself as a community on its fidelity to the Gospel and to the monastic way of life. It is called "Regular" because traditionally, a portion of the rule (from the Latin, *regula*) is read and commented on by the Prioress or another sisters delegated by her. Afterwards, if they so wish, the sisters may accuse themselves of external faults they may have committed against the common good of the community. Any proclamation of one nun by another is always to be excluded.

ABOUT THE DOMINICAN NUNS

Consecrated to life of prayer and praise, Dominican nuns share in the redemptive work of Christ in the heart of the Order of Preachers. In striving to live with one mind and heart in God, they seek to know and love God in the living of the traditional monastic observances of daily Holy Mass, chanted Divine Office, *lectio divina*, private prayer, study and work. The monastery also has the privilege of the *Adoring Rosary*—perpetual adoration of the Blessed Sacrament and the perpetual Rosary. The Dominican nun's life is one of hidden apostolic fruitfulness as she proclaims the Gospel of Christ by the witness of her life.

Women between the ages of 21-40 who are attracted to this way of life and would like more information are invited to contact us at:

Vocation Directress
Monastery of Our Lady of the Rosary
543 Springfield Avenue
Summit, NJ 07901-4498
908.273.1228
www.op.org/nunsopsumit
vocations.summit@op.org

For the **Amata Means Beloved** website:
www.AmataMeansBeloved.8m.com

0-595-30024-3

Printed in the United States
21237LVS00001BA/634-732